STEP-BY-STEP
EXPERIMENTS WITH
TASTE AND DIGESTION

By Katie Marsico

Illustrated by Bob Ostrom

The Child's World®

Published by The Child's World®
1980 Lookout Drive • Mankato, MN 56003-1705
800-599-READ • www.childsworld.com

ACKNOWLEDGMENTS
The Child's World®: Mary Berendes, Publishing Director
The Design Lab: Design and production
Red Line Editorial: Editorial direction
Consultant: Diane Bollen, Project Coordinator, Mars Rover Mission,
    Cornell University

ISBN 9781609736149
LCCN 2011940150

PHOTO CREDITS
Zsolt Biczó/Shutterstock Images, cover; Pilar Echeverria/Dreamstime,
cover, back cover; Jiri Vaclavek/Dreamstime, 1, 10; Tamara Kulikova/
Shutterstock Images, 4; Marco Mayer/Shutterstock Images, 8; Noam
Armonn/Shutterstock Images, 14; Dreamstime, 16; Artsem Martysiuk/
Shutterstock Images, 20; Africa Studio/Shutterstock Images, 24; Lisa F.
Young/Shutterstock Images, 25

Design elements: Pilar Echeverria/Dreamstime, Robisklp/Dreamstime,
Sarit Saliman/ Dreamstime, Jeffrey Van Daele/Dreamstime

Printed in the United States of America

BE SAFE!

The experiments in this book are meant for kids to do themselves. Sometimes an adult's help is needed though. Look in the supply list for each experiment. It will list if an adult is needed. Also, some supplies will need to be bought by an adult.

TABLE OF CONTENTS

4

We like to eat food that tastes good to us.

CHAPTER ONE

Study Taste and Digestion!

What foods do you like best? Maybe it is sweet ice cream. Or maybe it is salty pretzels. The flavor of food is what you like. How it smells or feels in your mouth is important, too. What you like is the way the food tastes!

What about the rest of your body? **Organs** break down the foods you eat. These organs include your stomach and **intestines**. This is called digestion. It breaks down food into different forms. The new forms are small enough to be used by your body. And your body needs food to create energy. Energy helps people stay healthy and grow.

Taste helps people enjoy the foods they eat. Digestion helps their bodies take **nutrients** from food. How can you learn more about taste and digestion?

CHAPTER TWO

Seven Science Steps

Doing a science **experiment** is a fun way to discover new facts! An experiment follows steps to find answers to science questions. This book has experiments to help you learn about taste and digestion. You will follow the same seven steps in each experiment:

Seven Steps

1. **Research**: Figure out the facts before you get started.
2. **Question**: What do you want to learn?
3. **Guess**: Make a **prediction**. What do you think will happen in the experiment?
4. **Gather**: Find the supplies you need for your experiment.
5. **Experiment**: Follow the directions.
6. **Review**: Look at the results of the experiment.
7. **Conclusion**: The experiment is done. Now it is time to reach a **conclusion**. Was your prediction right?

Are you ready to become a scientist? Let's experiment to learn about taste and digestion!

Does smell help us taste?

CHAPTER THREE

Does Your Nose Know?

Pizza smells so good. But does its smell make it taste better?
Find out if your nose changes how you taste food.

Research the Facts

Here are a few. What else do you know?

- Different foods have different smells.
- Air carries the smell of the food you are eating.

Ask Questions

- Does what you smell change what you taste?
- Do other organs besides your tongue help you taste?

Make a Prediction

Here are two examples:

- Your sense of smell changes what you taste.
- Your sense of smell does not change what you taste.

- Adult help
- Knife
- A banana
- A lemon
- A glass of water
- Pencil or pen
- Paper

Time to Experiment!

1. Ask an adult for help. Cut a few slices of the banana and lemon.
2. Pinch your nose shut. Breathe through your mouth. Now eat a sweet banana slice. What do you taste?
3. Let go of your nose. Eat another banana slice. Does it taste different now? Or does it taste the same? Write in your notes what happens.

4. Drink some water. It washes away the banana taste in your mouth.

5. Repeat steps 1 and 2 with a sour lemon slice. Remember to write in your notes.

6. Drink some water. It will wash the lemon taste from your mouth. Put the rest of the banana and lemon away.

Review the Results

Read your experiment notes. How did the foods taste when you could not smell them? You could not taste the foods well when you could not smell.

What Is Your Conclusion?

Did you predict the right answer? Smell changes taste. **Nerves** in your nose work with nerves in your mouth. They send messages to your brain. The messages tell you how food tastes. When you smell food it can make you hungry. Your brain knows about food even before you eat!

It is harder to taste flavors when you have a cold. A stuffy nose makes it harder to smell food.

14

Does saliva **help us taste food?**

CHAPTER FOUR

Why Is Spit So Special?

How does saliva, or spit, change taste? You will learn if a dry mouth changes the way your **taste buds** work.

Research the Facts

Here are a few. What else do you know?

- Saliva is the liquid in your mouth. Many people call it spit.
- Saliva helps us chew, swallow, and digest food.

Ask Questions

- Can you taste food with a dry mouth?
- Does food taste better in a wet mouth?

Make a Prediction

Here are two examples.

- Food will have less taste in a dry mouth.
- Food will taste the same in a dry or wet mouth.

Gather Your Supplies!

- 2 clean paper towels
- A cup of water
- A handful of pretzels
- Vinegar
- Spoon
- Pencil or pen
- Paper

Time to Experiment!

1. Wipe your tongue dry. Use a clean paper towel. Swallow a few times. This gets rid of extra saliva.

2. Eat a few pretzels. How does this salty food taste? Can you taste the pretzels? Write in your notes.

3. Drink some water. This makes your mouth wet again. Now eat a few pretzels. Do they taste the same? Write in your notes.

4. Repeats steps 1 to 3 with a spoonful of vinegar. Vinegar is **bitter.** It has a strong taste. Only try a little of it. Record what happens in your notes.

5. Now take a big drink of water. Put away any extra food.

Review the Results

Study your notes. Did taste change when your mouth was dry or wet? You should have tasted less with a dry mouth.

What Is Your Conclusion?

Saliva helps your taste buds work better. This makes you taste more. Taste buds cover your tongue. They do not work the right way unless they are wet. Saliva keeps your taste buds wet.

Saliva makes food soft. Food breaks down better. This is another way that saliva helps you taste!

Do different taste buds taste different foods better?

CHAPTER FIVE

What Is Your Tongue Telling You?

Do all taste buds work the same way? You will learn if some taste buds help you taste different flavors.

Research the Facts

Here are a few. What else do you know?

- There are five main flavors. They are bitter, salty, **savory**, sweet, and sour.
- Taste buds can detect the five main flavors.

Ask Questions

- Can some taste buds better detect certain flavors?
- Will a flavor taste the same on all parts of your tongue?

Make a Prediction

Here are two examples:

- Some taste buds better detect certain flavors.
- All taste buds detect flavors in the same way.

- 3 plastic cups
- Marker
- Water
- Measuring cup
- Measuring spoons
- Sugar
- Lemon juice
- 2 cotton swabs
- Pencil or pen
- Paper

Time to Experiment!

1. Pour 1 cup of water into each of the three cups. Number the cups 1, 2, and 3.

2. Mix 1 teaspoon of sugar into cup 1.

3. Mix 1 teaspoon of lemon juice into cup 2.

4. Dip a cotton swab into cup 1. Rub the cotton swab along the sides of your tongue. What do you taste? Write in your notes. Then take a sip of water from cup 3.

5. Repeat step 4. This time rub the cotton swab along the tip of your tongue. Do you taste anything different? Write in your notes. Take a sip of water from cup 3.

6. Repeat steps 4 and 5. Use the sour water from cup 2. Write in your notes what you taste.

7. Empty all three cups in the sink.

Review the Results

Read through your notes. Where did you taste the sweet water better? What about the sour water? The sweet taste was stronger on the tip of your tongue. The sour taste was stronger along the sides of your tongue.

What Is Your Conclusion?

Different taste buds detect different tastes better. The tongue's tip is better for sweet flavors. The tongue's sides are better for sour flavors. Taste buds on every part of your tongue detect all flavors. But some areas are better for certain flavors.

Scientists have created a tongue map. It shows what parts of the tongue better detect certain flavors.

Sweet watermelon is tasted better at the tip of the tongue.

CHAPTER SIX

Does Chewing Change Anything?

You have to chew your food. You do not want to choke! But what else does chewing food do? You will learn what chewing food does to digestion.

Research the Facts

Here are a few. What other facts do you know?

- Your body cannot digest large pieces of food.
- Your stomach contains an acid. Acid can break solids into small pieces.

You need to chew your food well.

Ask Questions

- Does chewing food help you digest it faster?
- Are small or large pieces of food more easily digested?

Make a Prediction

Here are two examples:
- Chewing food speeds up digestion.
- Chewing food slows down digestion.

Gather Your Supplies!

- Adult help
- 2 jars
- Vinegar
- Measuring cup
- 2 hard candies
- Hammer
- Pencil or pen
- Paper
- Camera (optional)

Time to Experiment!

1. Fill each jar with 1/2 cup of vinegar.
2. Next ask an adult for help. Smash one hard candy with a hammer.
3. Drop the broken candy into one jar. Then drop the whole candy into the other jar.
4. Check the jars every three minutes. Does one candy **dissolve** faster than the other? Write down what you see.
5. After 15 minutes, empty your jars in the sink. Throw away any candy that is left.

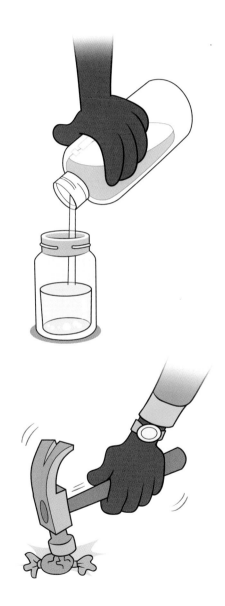

Review the Results

Study your notes. If you took pictures, look at them. How fast did the broken candy dissolve? How fast did the whole candy dissolve? The candies dissolved at different speeds. The broken candy dissolved faster.

What Is Your Conclusion?

The broken candy is like chewed food. The whole candy is like food that has not been chewed. Smaller pieces of food dissolve quickly. Bigger pieces of food dissolve slowly. Chewing breaks food into small pieces.

The acid in your stomach digests small pieces of food faster. The vinegar was like stomach acid. It took longer for the vinegar to dissolve the whole candy. It had to break down a large piece of food.

If you do not chew your food, it can cause health problems. Sometimes acid from your stomach goes into your throat. This can hurt. It can also harm your organs!

WAY TO GO!

Way to go! You are a scientist now. What fun taste and digestion facts did you learn? You found out that people use smell and saliva to taste the flavor of food. Then you saw how some parts of your tongue better detect flavors than others. You can learn even more about taste and digestion. Study it. Experiment with it. Then share what you learn about taste and digestion.

Glossary

bitter (BIT-ur): Something that taste harsh and sharp is bitter. Vinegar has a bitter taste.

conclusion (kuhn-KLOO-shuhn): A conclusion is what you learn from doing an experiment. Her conclusion is that saliva helps us taste.

dissolve (di-ZOLV): To dissolve is to seem to disappear when mixed with a liquid. Stomach acid helps food dissolve.

experiment (ek-SPER-uh-ment): An experiment is a test or way to study something to learn facts. The class did an experiment to learn about taste.

intestines (in-TESS-tinez): The intestines are the tubes that go from the stomach into the body and are used to digest food. Food moves through the intestines.

nerves (NURVZ): The nerves are fibers in your body that send messages to the brain and other body parts. Nerves in our tongues help us taste.

nutrients (NOO-tree-untz): Nutrients are things that people, animals, and plants need to stay alive. Food gives us nutrients to live.

organs (OR-guhnz): The organs are parts of the body that do certain jobs. Our stomach and intestines are organs used in digestion.

prediction (pri-DIKT-shun): A prediction is what you think will happen in the future. His prediction that taste buds need to be wet to taste better was right.

saliva (suh-LYE-vuh): Saliva is a clear liquid in the mouth that keeps it wet. Saliva helps us taste better.

savory (SAY-vuh-ree): Savory is a taste that is salty or spicy, but not sweet. Savory is one of the five main tastes.

taste buds (TAYST BUHDZ): Taste buds are cells on the tongue that taste if something is sweet, salty, sour, bitter, and savory. A tongue has many taste buds.

Books

Klingel, Cynthia, and Robert B. Noyed. *Mouth*. New York: Gareth Stevens Publishing, 2010.

Kurtz, John. *The World Around Us! Tasting*. Mineola, NY: Dover Publications, 2011.

Lennard, Kate. *Digestion*. Hauppauge, NY: Barrons Educational Series, Inc., 2009.

Web Sites

Visit our Web site for links about taste and digestion experiments: **childsworld.com/links**

Note to Parents, Teachers, and Librarians: We routinely verify our Web links to make sure they are safe and active sites. So encourage your readers to check them out!

Index

brain, 13
chewing, 15, 25, 26, 28
energy, 5
flavors, 5, 13, 21, 24, 29
intestines, 5
nerves, 13
nutrients, 5
organs, 5, 9, 28
saliva, 15, 17, 19, 29

smell, 5, 9, 13, 29
taste buds, 15, 19, 21, 24
tongue, 9, 17, 19, 21, 22, 23, 24, 29

ABOUT THE AUTHOR: Katie Marsico has written more than 80 books for children and young adults. She lives in Elmhurst, Illinois, with her husband and children.